MIDDLE SCHOOL
MISADVENTURES

MIDDLE SCHOOL
MISADVENTURES

PINK!

JASON PLATT

L B

LITTLE, BROWN AND COMPANY

NEW YORK BOSTON

ABOUT THIS BOOK

The illustrations for this book were done in Corel Painter on the Wacom Cintiq companion and colored in Adobe Photoshop. This book was edited by Russ Busse and designed by Christina Quintero. The production was supervised by Erika Schwartz, and the production editor was Annie McDonnell. The text was set in MisterAndMeBook, and the display type is MisterAndMe.

Little, Brown and Company
Hachette Book Group
1290 Avenue of the Americas, New York, NY 10104
Visit us at LBYR.com

First Edition: April 2019

Little, Brown and Company is a division of Hachette Book Group, Inc.
The Little, Brown name and logo are trademarks of Hachette Book Group, Inc.

The publisher is not responsible for websites (or their content) that are not owned by the publisher.

Library of Congress Cataloging-in-Publication Data
Names: Platt, Jason, author, illustrator.
Title: Middle school misadventures / by Jason Platt.
Description: First edition. | New York; Boston : Little, Brown and Company, 2019. | Summary: "In order to avoid extra work, middle schooler Newell agrees to participate in a school-wide talent show—without a talent"— Provided by publisher.
Identifiers: LCCN 2018033369| ISBN 9780316416863 (hardcover) | ISBN 9780316416887 (trade pbk.) | ISBN 9780316416870 (ebook) | ISBN 9780316528832 (library ebk. edition)
Subjects: LCSH: Graphic novels. | CYAC: Graphic novels. | Middle schools—Fiction. | Schools—Fiction. | Talent shows—Fiction. | Fathers and sons—Fiction.
Classification: LCC PZ7.7.P55 Mid 2019 | DDC 741.5/973—dc23
LC record available at https://lccn.loc.gov/2018033369

ISBNs: 978-0-316-41686-3 (hardcover), 978-0-316-41688-7 (pbk.), 978-0-316-41687-0 (ebook), 978-0-316-52967-9 (ebook), 978-0-316-53033-0 (ebook)

Printed in China

1010

Hardcover: 10 9 8 7 6 5 4 3 2 1
Paperback: 10 9 8 7 6 5 4 3 2 1

TO MY MOM, WHO ALWAYS MADE SURE I HAD
PAPER TO DRAW ON,

TO MY WIFE, WHO TOLD ME TO NEVER GIVE UP,

AND, ESPECIALLY TO MY SON—
WITHOUT HIM AND OUR ADVENTURES
THIS BOOK WOULD NOT BE IN YOUR HANDS.

* * *

I'M THE LUCKIEST GUY IN THE WORLD.

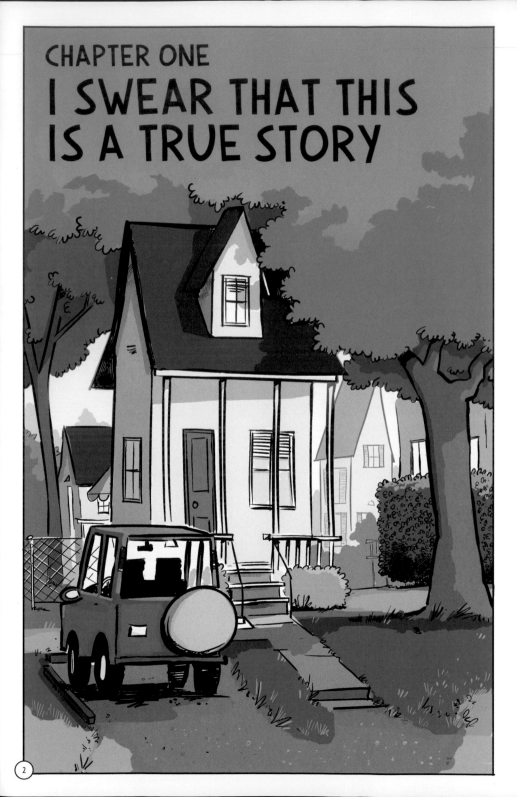

CHAPTER ONE
I SWEAR THAT THIS IS A TRUE STORY

3

WHAT AM I DOING HERE? COLLIN, WHAT ARE YOU TALKING ABOUT?

YOU'RE NOT MAKING ANY SENSE.

THINK **NEWELL,** THINK!!

COLLIN'S ALWAYS BEEN THE NERVOUS TYPE, BUT I'VE NEVER SEEN HIM LIKE THIS. HE ACTUALLY SOUNDS A LITTLE LIKE OUR HISTORY TEACHER, MR. JOHNSON.

HE'S ALWAYS ASKING THE SAME KIND OF PHILOSOPHICAL QUESTIONS DURING CLASS.

FLASH BACK!

HERE'S MY REPORT ON EGYPTIAN CULTURE, MR. JOHNSON. I'M SORRY IT'S LATE.

WHY AM I HERE?

THIS IS WHAT WE HAVE TO DEAL WITH ON A DAILY BASIS.

THE GIRLS IN CLASS THINK HE'S "DEEP." I THINK HE'S GONNA SNAP ANY DAY.

MR. JOHNSON I EXPECT TO BE ALL WEIRD, BUT NOT MY BEST FRIEND.

WHAT DO YOU MEAN?

WHY AREN'T YOU AT SCHOOL?

IT'S WEDNESDAY!?

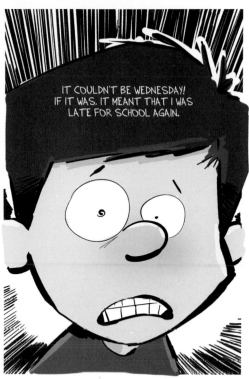

IT COULDN'T BE WEDNESDAY! IF IT WAS, IT MEANT THAT I WAS LATE FOR SCHOOL AGAIN.

THE LAST TIME I WAS LATE FOR SCHOOL OUR PRINCIPAL, MR. TODD, SAID...

FLASH BACK!

NEWELL,

IF YOU MISS **ONE** MORE CLASS, YOU WILL GO TO **SUMMER SCHOOL.**

SUMMER SCHOOL?

FART!!

DAGNABBIT, THIS CAN'T BE HAPPENING!

I CAN'T GET IT!

WHAT ARE WE GOING TO DO??

I DON'T KNOW! I'M WORKING ON IT!

WELL, WORK FASTER!

OKAY, LIFT YOUR ARMS UP, **NOW!**

WHAT DO YOU MEAN, LIFT UP MY ARMS?

31

33

I'LL JUST KEEP MY SUMMER SCHOOL SCHEDULE WITH ME FOR THE REST OF THE DAY.

JUST IN CASE.

AND I THOUGHT TODAY WAS GOING TO BE BORING.

I'M DEAD.

I HONESTLY DON'T KNOW HOW THIS DAY COULD GET ANY WORSE.

I MEAN, CAN IT?

CAN IT?

GASP! GASP!

TONK!

BY THE WAY, THE ANSWER IS YES. YES, IT COULD GET WORSE.

BUT THAT'S NOT EVEN THE BAD PART.

UM... NEWELL? YOU MIGHT WANT TO LOOK...

NO, THANK YOU. I'D RATHER STAY IN COMPLETE DENIAL.

NEWELL? CAN I SPEAK TO YOU FOR A MOMENT?

ANNNND OUT OF ALL THE BAD THINGS THAT HAPPENED THAT DAY, THAT RIGHT THERE WAS WHEN IT ALL WENT DOWNHILL. BELIEVE ME.

WHEN AN ADULT SAYS, "CAN I SPEAK TO YOU" YOU CAN BET THAT NOTHING GOOD WILL HAPPEN.

41

I'LL BE HONEST...THE NEXT FEW MINUTES WERE KIND OF A BLUR.

I FOLLOWED MR. TODD STRAIGHT TO HIS OFFICE.

GRUMBLE GRUMBLE GRUMBLE

I COULD STILL SMELL TOMMY'S SPAGHETTI ON HIM THE WHOLE WAY.

gulp!

THIS MIGHT BE HARD TO BELIEVE, BUT I HAD NEVER BEEN TO MR. TODD'S OFFICE BEFORE.

IT FELT LIKE I WAS WALKING INTO A LION'S DEN AND WAS ABOUT TO BE MAULED.

AND AS I SAT THERE...

I SLOWLY

STARTED

TO FREAK OUT.

NEWELL...

IT SEEMS THAT

SOMETIMES IT'S HARD TO FOLLOW WHAT ADULTS ARE TRYING TO TELL YOU.

THE ONLY THING YOU CAN DO IS RIDE THE WAVE. AND HOPE THAT YOU MAKE IT OUT OKAY.

YOU KNOW WHAT I MEAN?

BLAH BLAH BLAH BLAH

MR. TODD

43

I FELT SO EMPTY.

LIKE A STONE JUST FELL INTO MY STOMACH.

TonK

AND I WAS LEAVING MY BODY. AND I BECAME AN EMPTY NOTHING.

I DON'T REMEMBER EVEN HOW I GOT BACK TO THE CAFETERIA. THE THOUGHT OF NOT SEEING A SUMMER VACATION WAS ALL I COULD THINK ABOUT. MY FRIENDS WOULD LAUGH AT ME.

SO... GUESS WHO'S HAVING TO GO TO SUMMER SCHOOL NOW?

WHAT?

WHAT?

WHAT?

WHY DID I EVEN BOTHER?

NOT THAT I LOOK FORWARD TO HER MAKING FUN OF ME. BUT WHERE'S CLARA?

SHE RAN OFF IMMEDIATELY AFTER YOU WENT TO THE PRINCIPAL'S OFFICE.

I THINK SHE WENT TO THE BATHROOM OR SOMETHING.

YEAH, SHE SEEMED PRETTY UPSET.

EVEN WITHOUT THE WHOLE SUMMER SCHOOL THING, I'VE NEVER BEEN A MATH GUY.

WATCHING MISS TANNER EXPLAIN IT ALL ALWAYS LEAVES ME FEELING A LITTLE EXHAUSTED.

AND MAYBE A LITTLE DUMB...

SO IF YOU TAKE THE **BLAH BLAH BLAH** TAKE IT TO THE **BLAD-AH BLEE BLOO-BLOO.**

SQUEAK! SQUEAK! SQUEAK!

EVEN SKYLER, WHO IS OUR RESIDENT GENIUS, ALWAYS LEAVES MISS TANNER'S CLASS A LITTLE BAFFLED.

?

I CAN'T TELL YOU HOW MANY TIMES MISS TANNER HAS TOLD US THAT WHEN WE GROW UP WE WILL USE MATH EVERY DAY.

REMIND ME TO NEVER GROW UP, WILL YA?

LIFE WAS SO MUCH EASIER WHEN MATH WAS JUST ADDING AND SUBTRACTING.

SO WHEN THEY SAID WE WERE GOING TO DO MULTIPLICATION AND DIVISION, MY WHOLE WORLD GOT SHOOK UP A BIT.

ACTUALLY SAYING THAT IT SHOOK ME UP WAS PUTTING IT MILDLY. I FELT LIKE I WAS DROWNING.

I COULDN'T FIGURE ANY OF IT OUT.

AND BY THE TIME I DID...

THEY THREW ALGEBRA AT US.

PLOP!

FART.

OH...HELLO, MR. TODD, COME ON IN.

THANKS, MRS. GREENE. I'M SORRY TO INTERRUPT.

HELLO, STUDENTS!

I JUST WANTED TO PERSONALLY ANNOUNCE THAT GARFIELD MIDDLE SCHOOL WILL BE HOSTING ITS FIRST **TALENT SHOW** THIS **FRIDAY!**

TALENT SHOW? NO WAY. WHO'D EVER WANT TO DO SOMETHING LIKE THAT?

TALENT SHOW?!

TALENT SHOW?!

DO YOU HAVE A HIDDEN TALENT THAT YOU'VE ALWAYS WANTED TO SHOW OFF?

IN FRONT OF THE ENTIRE SCHOOL?

HMMMM... LET'S SEE. A CHANCE TO LOOK LIKE A COMPLETE IDIOT IN FRONT OF THE ENTIRE SCHOOL?

YEAH, RIGHT.

NOT ONLY IS IT A GREAT OPPORTUNITY FOR OUR TALENTED STUDENTS HERE...

OH! HOW EXCITING!

BUT AN EXCELLENT OPPORTUNITY FOR ANYONE WHO MIGHT BE HOPING TO GET OUT OF ANY DETENTION.

SO FOR THOSE WHO WANT TO WIPE THEIR SLATE COMPLETELY CLEAN, YOU MAY WANT TO TAKE ADVANTAGE OF THIS OPPORTUNITY, BECAUSE IT WILL ONLY BE OFFERED ONCE.

YES, SKYLER?

WOULD SUMMER SCHOOL KIDS QUALIFY FOR IT TOO?

SKYLER!

CRINGE

?

OH NO.

HA HA.

SIGH...

WELL, SKYLER, THANK YOU FOR ASKING. IF THERE WERE A PERSON WHO IS ATTENDING SUMMER SCHOOL AND THEY WERE TO BE THE FIRST ONE TO SIGN UP FOR THE TALENT SHOW, I MIGHT BE WILLING TO RECONSIDER.

BUT THAT PERSON BETTER ACT FAST.

AND THEIR NAME HAD BETTER BE FIRST ON THE SIGN-UP SHEET OUTSIDE OF THE OFFICE.

* HEH HEH HEH *

OH FART!

SHE KNOWS!

BRiiing!!

CLASS DISMISSED.

'SCUSE ME!

OUTTA MY WAY, PEOPLE!

GAH!! SHE'S GONNA SIGN IN FIRST!!

MOVE IT!

55

WELL, NEWELL... IT LOOKS LIKE WE HAVE OUR FIRST NAME ON OUR LIST.

RIP!

TALENT SHOW

GULP!

SHAKE SHAKE SHAKE

AND AM I READING THIS RIGHT?

THIS IS CERTAINLY EXCITING. I CAN'T WAIT TO SHARE THE NEWS WITH EVERYONE.

TALENT SHOW

MAYBE IT WAS THE EXCITEMENT OF RUNNING DOWN HERE, BUT I WASN'T UNDERSTANDING A WORD HE WAS SAYING.

TRUST ME... I'M JUST AS CONFUSED AS YOU ARE.

I WAS HESITANT WITH SKYLER'S REQUEST...BUT IF YOU'RE WILLING TO GO THROUGH WITH YOUR PROMISE, I WILL TOO. AS LONG AS YOU DO EVERYTHING THAT YOU SIGNED UP FOR, YOU WON'T HAVE TO GO TO SUMMER SCHOOL.

WAIT. WHAT?! MY NAME IS ON THE LIST?

THAT'S RIGHT. BUT IF YOU DON'T FULFILL YOUR PROMISE...WELL... LET'S JUST SAY THERE'S A SUMMER SCHOOL SEAT WITH YOUR NAME ON IT.

YOU DON'T HAVE TO WORRY ABOUT THAT, MR. TODD.

DON'T DISAPPOINT ME NOW!

I'LL TRY NOT TO.

SWING!

NO RUNNING!

PANT! PANT! PANT! PANT PANT! PANT PANT! PANT! PANT!

SLIDE

HA HA HA HA HA!! I DON'T KNOW ABOUT YOU, NEWELL...

BUT I MIGHT ACTUALLY BE EXCITED ABOUT THE TALENT SHOW NOW. HA HA HA HA HA!

I'M TRYING TO THINK...WHOSE LAUGH DOES HIS REMIND ME OF?

HA HA HA!

HA HA HA HA! I'M SO EXCITED ABOUT IT! I CAN'T WAIT! HA HA HA!

OH...NOW I REMEMBER.

YOU KNOW THAT FEELING YOU GET WHEN YOU THINK THAT PEOPLE ARE LAUGHING AT YOU AND NOT WITH YOU?

YEAH. THAT'S HIGH ON MY RADAR RIGHT NOW. WHATEVER IS GOING ON, IT CAN'T BE GOOD.

YOU SAID YOU'D GO AS A PENGUIN IN A TUTU?! **HA!** I CAN'T WAIT TO SEE THIS SHOW NOW!

SHAKE SHAKE SHAKE SHAKE SHAKE SHAKE SHAKE SHAKE SHAKE SHAKE SHAKE SHAKE SHAKE SHAKE SHAKE

HA! HA! HAHAHAHA HA! HA HA! HA HA!

SHAKE SHAKE SHAKE SHAKE SHAKE SHAKE SHAKE SHAKE SHAKE

UM...NEWELL?

SHAKE SHAKE SHAKE SHAKE SHAKE SHAKE SHAKE

ARE YOU OKAY?

GUYS? I THINK NEWELL'S ABOUT TO BLOW.

LD ?

SHAKE SHAKE SHAKE SHAKE SHAKE SHAKE SHAKE SHAKE SHAKE SHAKE SHAKE SHAKE

SO, EVERYONE, LISTEN...

NOBODY DO OR SAY ANYTHING THAT WILL MAKE HIM CRACK.

HAHA! HAHA!

CHAPTER FOUR
GRUMBLE

STOMP!

STOMP!

STOMP!

GRIN!

STARE

OBVIOUSLY YOU THINK THIS IS JUST ONE BIG JOKE.

NO. NO. NO. IT ISN'T!

I SWEAR!

DRESSED AS A PENGUIN WEARING A TUTU? ARE YOU EXPECTING ME TO TAKE THAT SERIOUSLY?

HA!

HA!

WELL, MRS. HENDRICKS, IT'S BEEN A LIFELONG DREAM OF MINE.

I'VE ALWAYS WANTED TO DRESS UP AS TEDDY ROOSEVELT SINGING "YOU'RE A GRAND OLD FLAG." BUT THAT WILL HAVE TO REMAIN MY UNREACHABLE DREAM.

I HATE TO BREAK IT TO YOU, NEWELL, BUT JUST DRESSING UP ISN'T CONSIDERED TO BE A TALENT. IT MIGHT MAKE YOU LOOK FOOLISH.

BUT BEING FOOLISH ISN'T CONSIDERED TALENT-WORTHY. WHAT ELSE DO YOU HAVE PLANNED FOR IT?

NOTHING YET.

83

IF YOU COULD PLEASE KEEP IT DOWN?

YEAH, NEWELL.

OH...SORRY. SORRY. SORRY.

YEESH.

SO I HAD TO WAIT AND WATCH AS EVERYONE ELSE SHOWED MRS. HENDRICKS WHAT THEY WERE GOING TO DO.

SIGH...

LA LA LA!

AND DURING THAT TIME, AS I WATCHED THEM ALL...

I WILL TAP DANCE WHILE RECITING THE PREAMBLE OF THE CONSTITUTION.

TAP TAP TAP!

I CAME TO REALIZE SOMETHING.

I'M GOING TO JUGGLE RUBBER CHICKENS.

EXCEPT FOR LILLY'S BALLET DANCING, EVERYONE ELSE'S TALENT WAS...

ACTUALLY KIND OF GOOFY.

I WILL BE DOING A MONOLOGUE FROM <u>HENRY V</u>.

I SPOKE TOO SOON.

BUT THEN I NOTICED...

EVEN AFTER THE BAD SINGING.

THE FUNNY

THE INTERESTING.

AND SNOOTY TALENTS...

MRS. HENDRICKS

SMILED

AND APPLAUDED

CLAP!
CLAP!
CLAP!

AFTER EACH ONE

HA!

OF THEM.

BRAVO!

*WIPE!

HECK, EVEN I COULD FIND SOMETHING THAT WOULD BE ON THAT SAME LEVEL!

I MIGHT BE ABLE TO DO THIS AFTER ALL!

BUT WHAT TO DO? THAT WAS THE NEXT BIG HURDLE.

THINK
THINK
THINK

OKAY...SO YOU'RE PROBABLY WONDERING WHY THE IDEA OF GOING DOWN THIS PARTICULAR STAIRWELL GIVES US THE WILLIES.

ON OUR FIRST DAY OF SCHOOL...

WE WERE ALL GATHERED IN THE CAFETERIA WHEN MR. TODD TOLD EVERYONE...

THE STAIRWELL ON THE EAST END OF THE SCHOOL IS **OFF LIMITS!!**

THIS VERY ONE RIGHT HERE.

FOR THE LONGEST TIME WE SPECULATED WHAT COULD HAVE BEEN DOWN THERE.

AND WE CAME UP WITH THE THREE BEST POSSIBLE REASONS WHY NO ONE WAS ALLOWED DOWN THERE.

AT NUMBER THREE: THAT AN OGRE WAS GUARDING ALL OUR GRADES.

GRADES DEPT.

WHICH DIDN'T SEEM LIKELY.

COMING IN AT NUMBER TWO:

VAMPIRES HAD RENTED THE SPACE OUT.

A LITTLE PRIVACY, PLEASE?

SWOON! WHICH ONLY MADE THE CUT BECAUSE THE GIRLS THOUGHT VAMPIRES WERE ROMANTIC FOR SOME REASON.

EYE ROLL

BUT THE NUMBER ONE GUESS WAS THE ONE THAT WE ALWAYS CAME BACK TO. WE FIGURED THAT

GANGSTERS FROM THE 1920S WERE BEING CHASED BY THE COPS AFTER A HEIST.

STOP IN THE NAME OF THE LAW!!

BAM! BAM! BAM!

BANG!

NOT TODAY, COPPERS!!

AND BURIED IT ALL BENEATH THE DIRT FLOOR.

WHERE IT REMAINED UNNOTICED AND UNTOUCHED.

FOR YEARS.

AND YEARS.

AND YEARS.

BRUSH BRUSH
BRUSH

AND WHEN MR. TODD SAW THE GANGSTERS' LOOT, HE COULDN'T RESIST IT.

HEH HEH HEH! I'M RICH!!

HE CLOSED OFF THE WAY DOWNSTAIRS.

AND TOLD ALL US KIDS...

THE STAIRWELL ON THE EAST END OF THE SCHOOL IS OFF LIMITS!!

AND HAS SPENT EVERY FREE MOMENT DIGGING UP THE REST OF THE BURIED TREASURE.

BUT TO MAKE SURE NO ONE CAME DOWN AND DISCOVERED WHAT HE WAS DOING...

HE EMPTIED OUT A BIG VAT OF SNAKES TO KEEP EVERYONE AWAY.

HISS HISS HISS HISS HISS HISS HISS HISS HISS HISS

AND IN THAT MOMENT I SAID SOMETHING REALLY, REALLY STUPID.

IT'S OKAY, GUYS. I'LL GO DOWN BY MYSELF.

I'LL LET YOU KNOW WHEN-IF-I MAKE IT.

REMEMBER ME.

WAIT... WHAT DID I SAY?

I'LL BE HONEST. I DON'T KNOW WHAT I WAS EXPECTING. MAYBE THAT SKYLER, LILLY, AND HECK EVEN CLARA WOULD CLAMOR AT ME, SAYING:

WHAT? NO!

DON'T GO, NEWELL!

DON'T BE A HERO!

TO SAVE ALL OF YOU, I MUST SACRIFICE MYSELF.

INSTEAD I GOT...

GOOD LUCK.

YEAH, GOOD LUCK, DUDE.

WOW... I'M FEELING THE LOVE, EVERYONE.

HISS
HISS
HISS HISS
HISS HISS
HISS
HISS HISS
HISS HISS
HISS HISS HISS HIS
HISS HISS HISS HISS
HISS HISS THISS HISS

AND THEY'LL ALL BE SITTING HERE WATCHING

YOU!

IT'S SO NICE BECAUSE IT CAN SEAT LITERALLY TEN TIMES AS MUCH AS THE CAFETERIA. ISN'T THAT AWESOME?!

TEN TIMES? HOW MANY PEOPLE IS THAT?

ONLY 500 PEOPLE.

ONLY 500?

500? OH MY! I DIDN'T KNOW IT WAS THAT MANY PEOPLE! HOW EXCITING!

DO YOU KNOW WHAT TEDDY ROOSEVELT WOULD SAY AT A TIME LIKE THIS?

BULLY!! HA HA!!

NOT EVEN HOUDINI COULD ESCAPE
500 PAIRS OF EYES STARING AT
HIM, OR EVEN ESCAPE THE SOUNDS
OF THEIR LAUGHTER. ADULTS LOVE
TELLING US KIDS THAT FACING OUR
FEARS BUILDS UP CHARACTER.

BUT I'M PRETTY SURE THAT NONE OF THESE GROWN-UPS WOULD GO THROUGH THE SAME CHARACTER-BUILDING OPPORTUNITY.

BOOM!

ESPECIALLY IF THE CHARACTER BUILDING INVOLVED THEM DRESSING UP AS A PENGUIN WEARING A TUTU.

HUMILIATING.

LATER

OH.. WELL THEN, YOU WOULDN'T MIND TRADING PLACES WITH ME, WOULD YA?

NO-NO-NO. I DIDN'T SAY THAT.

I'M SORRY THAT YOU GOT ROPED INTO DOING IT TOO.

IT'S NOT YOUR FAULT. WHAT'S THE SAYING "I WAS IN THE WRONG PLACE AT THE WRONG TIME?"

ANY IDEA WHAT YOU'RE GOING TO DO FOR IT?

NONE. BUT I'LL FIGURE SOMETHING OUT. I'M SURE. THIS IS KINDA LIKE DOING A SCIENCE PROJECT. I DON'T WORRY ABOUT BEING THE NEXT EINSTEIN. I JUST NEED TO THINK ABOUT WHAT THEY WANT TO SEE AND GET IT DONE AND OVER WITH.

I'LL PROBABLY SING A SONG OR SOMETHING LIKE THAT.

SNICKER SNICKER YOU? SING SOMETHING? SNICKER SNICKER

HA! HA! HA!

AHEM.

REALLY? LAUGHING AT THE IDEA OF ME SINGING? REALLY? DO THE WORDS PENGUIN AND TUTU RING A BELL WITH YOU, NEWELL?

BLINK BLINK

YOU'RE RIGHT. I'M SORRY. I JUST NEEDED TO LAUGH AT SOMETHING BESIDES EVERYONE LAUGHING AT ME, I GUESS.

NO PROBLEM, I GET IT.

I NEED TO RUN AND FIGURE OUT WHAT I'M GONNA DO FOR THE TALENT SHOW. I'LL SEE YOU TOMORROW. WHICH IS THURSDAY, BY THE WAY!!

YOU'RE SOOOOOOO FUNNY! HAR HAR HAR!

118

I KNOW THAT TOMORROW'S THURSDAY! I'M NOT STUPID!

SO IF TOMORROW IS THURSDAY, THEN THAT MAKES TODAY...

WEDNESDAY

THURSDAY
MAY 22nd

FRIDAY
MAY 23rd

THE TALENT SHOW!!

CRAP! FRIDAY WAS CLOSER THAN I THOUGHT! I NEEDED TO FIGURE OUT WHAT I WAS GOING TO DO, FAST!

AAAAAAAAH!

YOU CAN RUN ALL YOU WANT, NEWELL! BUT I'M CATCHING UP WITH YOU QUICK!

FRIDAY
MAY 23rd
THE TALENT SHOW

I COULD FEEL FRIDAY CLOSING IN ON ME.

I HATE ASKING FOR HELP.

IT MAKES ME FEEL TOO MUCH LIKE A LITTLE KID.

BUT SOMETIMES YOU JUST HAVE TO SWALLOW YOUR PRIDE AND KNOW WHEN TO ASK FOR IT.

PANT!
PANT!
PANT!

DAD?!

119

WELL?

WELL... IT'S AH... I'M KINDA OF, AH

SPIT IT OUT.

SO I DID.

I TOLD HIM THE WHOLE STORY.

ABOUT COLLIN AND ME RUNNING TO SCHOOL.

MAKING FUN OF MR. TODD... AND GETTING CAUGHT.

DOOPTY DURR

ABOUT HAVING TO ATTEND SUMMER SCHOOL. WHICH HE DIDN'T EVEN BLINK AT, AND THE HALLWAY CHASE WITH CLARA.

!

THE WHOLE TIME MY DAD'S ARMS WERE CROSSED AND HIS LEFT FOOT KEPT TAPPING. A SURE SIGN THAT HE WASN'T HAPPY.

SO...

TAP! TAP! TAP!

HAVE TO PERFORM IN THE SCHOOL'S TALENT SHOW THIS FRIDAY.

THE TALENT SHOW, HUH?

OH MAN... HERE IT COMES.

SIGH...

NEWELL, I DON'T KNOW WHAT TO SAY, EXCEPT...

THAT'S AWESOME!!

yeesh...

I KNEW HE'D BE EXCITED ABOUT IT. THAT'S EXACTLY WHY I WAS HESITANT IN TELLING HIM ABOUT THIS WHOLE MESS.

AW, MAN! THIS IS GONNA BE GREAT!

GREAT.

UM, DAD?

I'LL HAVE TO SEND OUT INVITES!

HOW EXCITING!

OOOH! YOU KNOW WHAT WE CAN DO?

WE CAN HOST AN AFTERPARTY HERE AT THE HOUSE!

WOULDN'T THAT BE COOL?!

PLEASE DON'T.

THIS IS GONNA BE INCREDIBLE.

WOW!! I NEED TO FIND THE VIDEO CAMERA.

THE VIDEO CAMERA? GREAT.

I HAVE SO MUCH TO DO BEFORE FRIDAY!

I FIGURED THIS WAS GOING TO HAPPEN. SEE, MY DAD USED TO DO THE MUSICALS WAY BACK WHEN HE WAS IN HIGH SCHOOL.

THAT'S HIM THERE.

SPORTING THE MUSTACHE. THIS WAS LIKE A BILLION YEARS AGO. HE TOLD ME SO.

HE PROBABLY THINKS THAT I'M LIVING OUT HIS GLORY DAYS OR SOMETHING.

HOPEFULLY WITHOUT HAVING TO GROW OUT ANY FACIAL HAIR. YUCK!!

WAIT! I THINK I KNOW WHERE THE CAMERA IS!

UM, DAD?

DAD?

OOOF!

WAAAAAAA!!

SKRK!

WOW...SORRY, DAD. I DID NOT MEAN FOR THAT TO HAPPEN.

NAH, IT'S ALL GOOD. THE CARPET BURN STINGS AND I'LL BE SORE IN THE MORNING, BUT I'M OKAY.

SO YOU NEED SOME HELP FIGURING OUT WHAT TO DO FOR THE TALENT SHOW?

BIG TIME. AND NOT ONLY THAT, BUT I HAVE TO BE DRESSED IN A PENGUIN SUIT WEARING A TUTU.

?

WHAT?! NO—NOT BY CHOICE.

OKAY, OKAY. I WASN'T JUDGING. I DON'T KNOW WHAT THE TRENDS ARE NOWADAYS.

AS FAR AS I KNOW, IT'S THE "IN" THING THESE DAYS.

A PENGUIN SUIT AND A TUTU TRENDY? COME ON, DAD.

WELL, I DON'T KNOW.

YOU SHOULD HAVE SEEN WHAT KIDS WERE WEARING WHEN I WAS YOUR AGE.

THAT SOUNDS SCARY.

I JUST NEED TO FIGURE OUT WHAT TO DO. BECAUSE I DON'T HAVE A TALENT.

WHAT? OF COURSE YOU HAVE A TALENT.

OH YEAH? LIKE WHAT?

THAT'S EASY.

· · ·

· · ·

THIS ISN'T ENCOURAGING.

OOOH! WAIT! I HAVE SOME OLD STUFF IN THE ATTIC THAT MIGHT BE ABLE TO HELP YOU OUT!

THE ATTIC?

YEAH! WHY DIDN'T I THINK OF IT BEFORE!

THE ATTIC?

KNOCK! KNOCK! KNOCK!

YEAH! THE ATTIC! WHAT'S THE BIG DEAL?

125

NO BIG DEAL. IF YOU DON'T MIND CREEPY-CRAWLY PLACES.

HELLO?

OH, COME ON IN, COLLIN.

HEY, NEWELL. HOW'S IT COMING ALONG?

WHAT ARE YOU DOING HERE? DON'T YOU NEED TO FIGURE OUT WHAT YOU'RE GONNA DO?

I TOLD YA. I GOT THAT ALL FIGURED OUT. I'M GONNA SING A SONG. SOMETHING I ALREADY KNOW.

I'LL BE IN-OUT AND OUTTASIGHT, LICKETY-SPLIT.

WHAT ABOUT YOU? YOU FIGURE OUT WHAT YOU'RE GONNA DO YET?

I'M, AH... I'M WEIGHING MY OPTIONS RIGHT NOW.

OH YEAH? WHAT OPTIONS ARE YOU THINKIN' ABOUT?

WELL, TELL ME WHAT YOU THINK.

THIS OUGHT TO BE INTERESTING.

AND WHILE I'M SOAKING UP THE PACIFIC SUN...

SQUAAK!

SQWAAA!

MR. TODD HAS GONE CRAZY SEARCHING THE GLOBE TRYING TO FIND ME.

NEWELL!

TO LONDON.

HMMM...

EGYPT.

WHERE ARE YOU?

AND TO THE GREAT WALL OF CHINA.

I'LL FIND YOU!!

AND FINALLY, IF MY PLAN WORKS OUT AS WELL AS I THINK IT WILL... MR. TODD WILL LOSE HIS MIND.

MAYBE NEWELL WILL BE HERE! DO YOU THINK?

I'M SURE HE WILL BE, MR. TODD. I'M SURE HE WILL BE.

AND I WILL BE FREE FROM THE TALENT SHOW FOREVER!

FOREVER?!

MWA HA! HA HA HA!! HA!

WHAT?

I DON'T THINK YOU CAN JUST JOIN THE WITNESS PROTECTION PROGRAM.

IT'S NOT LIKE JOINING THE SCOUTS.

YEAH, I HEAR THAT IF YOU'RE IN THE PROGRAM YOU'RE JUST AN AVERAGE NOBODY. AND YOU GET EGG NOODLES AND KETCHUP INSTEAD OF SPAGHETTI.

FART.

PLUS, IT'S NOT VERY COOL TO MAKE SOMEONE LOSE THEIR MIND LIKE THAT.

WELL, IT'S GOOD TO KNOW THAT YOU'RE CONCERNED ABOUT OUR PRINCIPAL'S MENTAL WELL-BEING WHILE YOUR BEST FRIEND IS LOSING HIS OWN MARBLES!

WELL, IF YOU WEREN'T LATE TO SCHOOL ALL THE TIME YOU MIGHT NOT BE IN THIS MESS!

OH! SO THIS IS ALL MY FAULT, HUH?

SORRY.

YOU SHOULD BE.

NEWELL.

SIGH... I'M SORRY TOO.

THERE... DOESN'T THAT MAKE YOU FEEL BETTER?

WHY DO GROWN-UPS ALWAYS SAY THAT? MAYBE FEELING AWKWARD IS THE SAME THING AS FEELING BETTER. WHO KNOWS.

WELL, YOU TRY AND FIGURE OUT WHAT YOU'RE GONNA DO FOR THE TALENT SHOW, AND I'LL FIGURE OUT WHAT TO DO ABOUT THE COSTUME.

WISH ME LUCK.

BAM!

SEE YA.

BYE, DAD! AND THANKS!

...

...

SO, WHAT'S UP IN THE ATTIC?

MY DAD THINKS THAT SOME OF HIS OLD STUFF MIGHT HELP ME FIGURE OUT WHAT I CAN DO.

CAN YOU HELP? OR ARE YOU GONNA GO BACK HOME?

SURE. I'LL HELP. I'M UP FOR AN ADVENTURE.

WHEW!! I REALLY DON'T LIKE GOING UP THERE!!

133

CREAK!

ALL RIGHT... HERE WE GO.

OH...I SEE WHAT YOU MEAN.

OUR ATTIC IS ONE OF THOSE WALK-UP KINDS. WHAT KIND OF ATTIC IS THIS?

THE HORROR-MOVIE KIND.

WELP. HERE GOES NOTHIN'.

ANNNND JUST WHAT I THOUGHT.

CREEPY TOWN.

SEE ANYTHING YET?

NOT REALLY. JUST SOME OLD COSTUME-TYPE STUFF.

NOT SURE IF I CAN DO ANYTHING WITH IT, BUT I'LL PUT IT ASIDE JUST IN CASE.

HEY! CHECK THIS OUT!

TADA!

I'M COLLIN THE MAGNIFICENT!

WHOA! THAT'S AWESOME!

I FEEL SO ELOQUENT WEARING THIS.

WHAT ELSE IS IN HERE?

ANYTHING THAT CAN HELP?

TINK! TINK!

IT'S LIKE A WHOLE MAGIC SHOP IN HERE! WE GOT SOME SORT OF MAGIC RINGS HERE.

OOOOOOOOOH!! A MAGIC WAND.

AND A DECK OF MAGIC CARDS.

AH, YES. I RECOGNIZE THIS ONE. NO GOOD MAGICIAN IS COMPLETE WITHOUT KNOWING THE CLASSIC 52 PICKUP TRICK.

IS THERE ANYTHING ELSE IN THERE THAT YOU CAN MAKE A MESS WITH?

I DON'T KNOW. LEMME CHECK.

I WAS BEING SARCASTIC.

THERE'S TONS OF OTHER STUFF IN HERE, DUDE.

OH YEAH, LIKE WHAT?

LIKE MY DAD'S VHS COPY OF "HOW TO BREAKDANCE IN 12 EASY STEPS".

YEAH, I THINK WE'RE ALL DONE HERE.

TOTALLY. THE THOUGHT OF MY DAD TRYING TO BE HIP IS DISTURBING.

OKAY, DO YOU THINK THIS IS ENOUGH TO START WITH?

YEAH, I THINK SO. WHEW! I WANT TO BE DONE. IT'S HOT UP HERE.

HERE'S WHAT WE'LL DO.

YOU GET ON THE LADDER, AND I'LL LOWER THE BOXES. HOW'S THAT SOUND?

THAT'S FINE. JUST DON'T FALL ON ME.

I MAKE NO PROMISES.

YOU KNOW, IT'S NOT EASY BEING YOUR FRIEND.

I SHOULD GET PAID FOR IT.

HARDE HAR HAR!

I'M SERIOUS.

SIGH...

THERE IS ONLY ONE THING THAT CAN HELP ME NOW.

AWESOME MIX!!

AWESOME MIX!

AWESOME MIX!

CLICK!

AT TIMES LIKE THIS, I GO RETRO AND PULL OUT SOME OF MY DAD'S OLD MIX TAPES.

AND THEN HAVE MYSELF...

WHUR WHUR WHUR...

AN OLD-FASHIONED HERO TRAINING MONTAGE!!

DOO DOO BAH DEE BAH DOO-BAH DEE-DOO! DOO!

CHAPTER NINE
PROCRASTINATION STATION

WAIT... SO THE HERO TRAINING MONTAGE DIDN'T HELP?

NOT THIS TIME, NO.

I'M SURPRISED.

ME TOO. IT STINKS BECAUSE THAT WAS MY GO-TO SONG.

WHO KNEW THAT THOSE OLD TAPES HAD SO MUCH TAPE IN THEM! IT TOOK OVER AN HOUR TO CUT MYSELF FREE FROM IT ALL.

164

HAHAHAHA!!A!

I THINK THAT'S THE BEST ONE YET!

I TOTALLY AGREE! I

AHEM!

THAT WAS COOL AND ALL, BUT YOU'RE KINDA BLOCKING THE STAIRS.

WHAT?

OH... SORRY.

SORRY.

SORRY, MADDIE.

YOU KNOW, WE SHOULD PROBABLY BE MORE AWARE WHEN WE DO OUR HANDSHAKE FROM NOW ON.

GEE, NEWELL, YA THINK?

HRUMPH!

HA HA! THANKS FOR YOUR OPINION, RAUL! I DIDN'T ASK FOR IT!

HEY!

YOU TWO GETTING IN TROUBLE AGAIN?

NO, NOT REALLY. COLLIN AND I WERE DOING OUR HANDSHAKE AND WE KINDA GOT IN THE WAY.

OH, THE FAMOUS NEWELL AND COLLIN HANDSHAKE. WHAT DID YOU GUYS SHAKE ON THIS TIME?

NEWELL AND I BASICALLY SWORE OFF GIRLS. THEY'RE TOO MUCH TROUBLE.

TOO MUCH TROUBLE?!?

NO NO NO NO NO NO! I DIDN'T MEAN IT LIKE THAT!

OH??

SO WHAT DO YOU MEAN?

YEAH! WHAT DO YOU MEAN?

I—AH— I WAS JUST— I DIDN'T—I MEAN, I, OR WE HUMMANA HUMMANA.

IT'S OKAY, NEWELL.

REALLY. I WILL TAKE INTO CONSIDERATION THAT WHAT YOU SAID WAS YOUTHFUL IGNORANCE AND TAKE IT WITH A GRAIN OF SALT.

BUT IF GIRLS ARE TOO MUCH TROUBLE...

I GUESS I KNOW WHO I'M NOT GOING TO ASK TO SADIE HAWKIN'S...

WHAT'S A SADIE HAWKIN'S?

I DON'T KNOW. I WAS GOING TO ASK YOU THE SAME QUESTION.

SADIE HAWKIN'S IS A DANCE WHERE THE GIRL ASKS THE BOY, INSTEAD OF THE OTHER WAY AROUND.

IT'S LATER THIS SCHOOL YEAR.

FACE IT, DUDE. YOU BLEW IT.

BIG TIME.

? ?

MAN...HOW DOES HE DO IT?

DO YOU GET THE FEELING THAT ALL ROGER DOES IS WALK AROUND THE SCHOOL WAITING TO GIVE ME CRYPTIC ADVICE ABOUT GIRLS?

LIKE I DON'T FEEL AWKWARD ENOUGH AROUND THEM AS IT IS, YOU KNOW?

HE'S LIKE A PROPHET THAT WAY...OR A SITH LORD.

DEFINITELY ONE OF THE TWO. FOR SURE.

BUT WHAT DOES HE MEAN THAT I BLEW IT? DOES HE MEAN WITH SKYLER?

DUH!

I'LL TELL YOU WHAT, LOVER BOY. IF SKYLER WON'T ASK YOU OUT TO THE SADIE HAWKIN'S DANCE, YOU CAN BE MY DATE WHEN THE TIME COMES!

OooOoooOh! I CAN SEE IT NOW.

IT'LL BE A MAGICAL NIGHT, NEWELL!

I'LL WEAR A BIG POOFY DRESS, AND YOU CAN WEAR A TIE. IT'LL BE A NIGHT WE WON'T FORGET!

SKYLER'S LOSS WILL BE YOUR GAIN!

HA! HA! HA! HA! HA! HA! HA! HA! HA! HA HA! HA! HA HA! HA! HA HA

I'D RATHER PERFORM IN TWO STUPID **TALENT SHOWS** THAN GO TO A DANCE WITH YOU, CLARA!

DON'T LET HER GET TO YOU. YOU GOT THE TALENT SHOW TO WORRY ABOUT FIRST.

YOU HAVE MONTHS TO WORRY ABOUT THE DANCE. AND POSSIBLY FAKE YOUR OWN DEATH.

PANT! PANT! PANT! PANT! PANT!

YOU'RE RIGHT. SHE'S TRYING TO MAKE ME LOSE FOCUS. I HAVE TO CONCENTRATE ON THE TALENT SHOW. I'M NOT GOING TO LOOK LIKE AN IDIOT.

SMAK!

AND BEFORE YOU CAN SAY ANYTHING.

YES... I CAUGHT THE IRONY IN THAT LAST STATEMENT.

SNICKER SNICKER

I'M GLAD YOU SAID IT AND NOT ME.

169

BRIGHT IDEA MOMENT!

BUT THEN I REALIZED...

IF I SPENT THE FIRST FEW MINUTES ASKING QUESTIONS,

VOLUNTEERING TO READ OUT LOUD,

AND GOING UP TO THE BOARD TO SOLVE AN ALGEBRA PROBLEM...

$X^2 + 40X 39 =$

HMM..

THE TEACHER WOULD THINK THAT I WAS PAYING ATTENTION!

LEAVING ME THE REST OF THE PERIOD TO CONCENTRATE ON THE TALENT SHOW!

BUT IT DIDN'T TAKE ME LONG TO FIGURE OUT THAT MY BRILLIANT PLAN HAD ONLY ONE MAJOR FLAW IN IT.

BECAUSE, BEFORE I KNEW IT...

BRiiiNG!

CLASS WAS OVER.

AND BECAUSE I SPENT TOO MUCH TIME ACTUALLY WORKING IN THE CLASS, I DIDN'T GET A SINGLE MOMENT TO EVEN THINK ABOUT ANYTHING ELSE.

BUMMER, RIGHT?

EXCELLENT PARTICIPATION TODAY, NEWELL!

I KNOW. I'M DISAPPOINTED IN MYSELF TOO.

MATH ADD IT UP! IT'S FUN!

CLARA!

WHAT?

YOU CAN'T JUST TAKE HIS SANDWICH LIKE THAT!

WHAT? HE WASN'T GONNA EAT IT.

AND WHAT DO YOU CARE? I THOUGHT YOU WERE MAD AT HIM!

THANKS, GUYS. BUT, SERIOUSLY, SHE CAN HAVE IT. I'M NOT THAT HUNGRY.

SEE?

WHAT'S GOING ON? YOU SICK OR SOMETHING?

NOPE. HE STILL CAN'T THINK OF WHAT TO DO FOR THE TALENT SHOW TOMORROW.

WHAT?

WHAT?

YOU KNOW IT'S TOMORROW, RIGHT?

UGH.

HA!

AND BELIEVE ME... WHEN YOU'RE BEING SURROUNDED BY NOTHING BUT TICKING CLOCKS, YOU CAN'T CONCENTRATE ON ANYTHING ELSE.

AND BEFORE I KNEW IT...

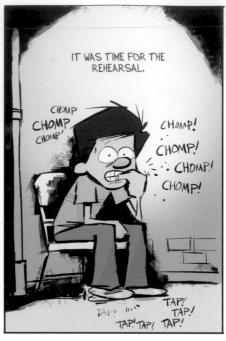

IT WAS TIME FOR THE REHEARSAL.

SO I WAITED IN WHAT THEY WERE CALLING THE WINGS AND WATCHED THE OTHERS REHEARSE THEIR TALENT FOR MRS. HENDRICKS.

I WAS SECRETLY HOPING THAT WATCHING THEM REHEARSE WOULD MAKE ME FEEL GOOD ABOUT WHERE I WAS.

SLAP!

BUT AS I WATCHED THEM...

I REALIZED THEY WEREN'T AWKWARD AT ALL.

THEY WERE GOOD. REALLY, REALLY GOOD. AWESOME, EVEN.

SO INSTEAD OF FEELING GOOD, IT MADE ME FEEL WORSE THAN EVER.

TAP
TAP TAP
TAP
TAP
TAP
TAP
TAP
TAP TAP
TAP
TAP TAP

AND THEN...

WELL, THIS OUGHTA BE INTERESTING... NEWELL? YOU'RE NEXT!

FART.

WHAT WAS THAT?

NOTHING! I'M COMING!

MIMICKING EVERYONE ELSE, I WALKED UP TO THE SPOT ON THE STAGE WHERE THEY STOOD. IT WAS WEIRD. AS I WALKED UP OR DOWN, WHATEVER THEY SAID IT WAS, TIME SEEMED TO SLOW DOWN TO A CRAWL. AND YET, AT THE SAME TIME, MY HEART WAS RACING LIKE IT WAS TRYING TO WIN A GOLD MEDAL AT THE OLYMPICS.

FROM THE OTHER SIDE OF THE WINGS, I COULD FEEL THE EYES OF MY FRIENDS BURROW INTO ME.

WALKING UP TO THE EDGE OF THE STAGE I CAME TO THE CONCLUSION THAT THIS IS WHAT FACING DEATH MUST BE LIKE.

NO OFFENSE, MRS. HENDRICKS.

OKAY, FEEL FREE TO START WHENEVER YOU'RE READY.

OKAY.

TIME MIGHT HAVE BEEN GOING IN SLOW MOTION. BUT IT WASN'T GOING AS SLOW AS I WOULD HAVE LIKED IT. SO I DID THE ONLY THING I COULD THINK OF. I STALLED.

COUGH!
COUGH
COUGH

IT'S LIKE WATCHING A FISH OUT OF WATER AND I CAN'T DO ANYTHING TO HELP IT.

KOFF! COUGH! KOFF!

UGH!

I CAN'T WATCH.

DOES ANYONE HAVE ANY POPCORN?

COUGH! KOFF! COUGH

WHAT ?!?

IT'S ENTERTAINING.

ANYTIME, NEWELL. WE STILL HAVE MARTIN'S TALENT TO REHEARSE.

COUGH! KOFF! COUGH!

COUGH! KOFF!

COUGH KOFF

MAN! IF LOOKS COULD KILL! WHAT WAS MARTIN'S DEAL ANYWAY?

COUGH!!

NEWELL? I'M STARTING TO LOSE MY PATIENCE.

ONE COUGH MOMENT!

179

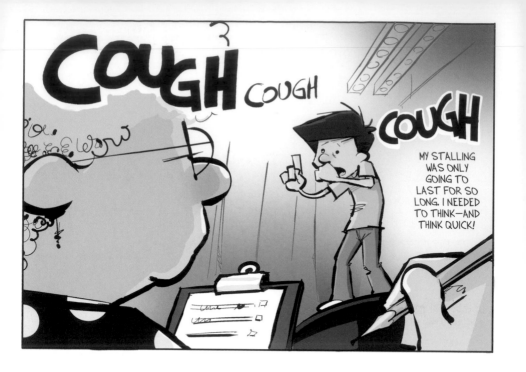

COUGH COUGH COUGH

MY STALLING WAS ONLY GOING TO LAST FOR SO LONG. I NEEDED TO THINK—AND THINK QUICK!

SO IN MY HEAD I DIVED INTO ALL THE BOXES THAT COLLIN AND I BROUGHT DOWN FROM THE ATTIC.

BUT I HAD GONE THROUGH THEM A MILLION TIMES ALREADY AND NOTHING—AND I MEAN NOTHING—WAS JUMPING OUT AT ME. I DIDN'T HAVE ANYTHING.

NNOOOO!

THIS SIDE UP

THE PROBLEM NOW WAS THAT I COULDN'T STOP COUGHING IF I TRIED. IT BECAME MORE OF A GAGGING THAN A COUGH.

COUGH! COFF! KOFF! COUGH

SIGH! OKAY! I SEE WHERE THIS IS GOING.

I CAN SEE THAT YOU'RE NOT TAKING THIS WHOLE TALENT SHOW SERIOUSLY, NEWELL. I'M GOING TO HAVE TO RECOMMEND TO MR. TODD THAT YOU'RE JUST...

COUGH COUGH

...NOT LIVING UP TO YOUR END OF THE AGREEMENT.

PLEASE! NO NO NO! I AM COUGH TAKING IT SERIOUSLY!

I CAN'T COUGH STOP COFF!! COUGHING!

COUGH COUGH KOFF

COME ON OUT, MARTIN. I'M SORRY THAT YOU HAD TO WAIT SO LONG.

AFTER THIS I HAVE SOME NEWS TO SHARE WITH MR. TODD. DON'T I, NEWELL?

YOU CAN COUNT ON ME, MRS. H!

NO, WAIT!! COUGH! I CAN COFF DO IT! KOFF COUGH COUGH COUGH PLEASE!

PLEASE, MRS. HENDRICKS! COUGH!! I DON'T KNOW IF IT'S NERVES OR COUGH!! BUT I HAVEN'T KOFF KOFF!! COUGHED ALL DAY.

MAYBE IT'S KOFF!! NERVES OR SOMETHING. I DON'T COUGH KNOW.

BUT I PROMISE YOU THAT COUGH! I HAVE BEEN WORKING ON COFF!! THIS TALENT SHOW NONSTOP!

PLEASE...

IT'S TRUE, MRS. HENDRICKS. I'VE EVEN HELPED HIM.

HE'S BEEN WORRYING ABOUT IT ALL DAY.

IT'S TRUE!

YUP!

WELL, NEWELL...

MRS. HENDRICKS KEPT TALKING, BUT I COULDN'T HEAR A WORD SHE SAID. IT WAS LIKE SHE WAS A MILLION MILES AWAY. AND SUDDENLY EVERYTHING WAS COMING UP TO THE SURFACE.

BLAH BLAH BLAH!

HO'BOY...

DEALING WITH THE THOUGHT OF GOING TO SUMMER SCHOOL. RACING CLARA TO THE SIGN-UP SHEET. DEALING WITH HAVING TO PERFORM IN THE TALENT SHOW WHILE DRESSED UP LIKE A PENGUIN WEARING A TUTU. GETTING INTO A FIGHT WITH MY BEST FRIEND. SURVIVING A SQUIRREL ATTACK. TRYING TO THINK OF SOMETHING— ANYTHING—TO DO FOR THIS SHOW. AND NOW THIS...I TELL YA. SOMETHING HAD TO GIVE.

?

OH, GREAT... HE'S GONNA START THE COUGHING BIT AGAIN.

WHILE I DID OPEN MY MOUTH...

I DIDN'T HAVE TO COUGH.

MMF!

MMMH!

AAAA!

!

HMMFLAGH!!!!

DID NEWELL JUST?

YUP...

ALL OVER MARTIN?

YUP.

...I'M GLAD I DIDN'T HAVE ANY POPCORN.

CHAPTER TEN

ICY METAPHORS

OKAY, THANKS, MRS. HIGGINS! I'LL MAKE SURE TO REST.

WHEW!

WHAT HAPPENED?

ARE YOU FEELING OKAY NOW?

DID YOU GET INTO TROUBLE AGAIN?

I GOT TO ADMIT IT, DUDE. WHAT HAPPENED WAS PRETTY GROSS, BUT AT THE SAME TIME KINDA AWESOME TOO.

WELL, A COUPLE OF THINGS. MRS. HIGGINS DOESN'T THINK I'M SICK,

BUT SHE DOESN'T WANT ME COMING INTO SCHOOL TOMORROW.

OH! SO DOES THAT MEAN YOU DON'T HAVE TO DO THE TALENT SHOW NOW?

CREAK!

THE ANSWER IS YES. YES HE DOES. AGAINST MY OWN JUDGMENT, MRS. HIGGINS WANTS YOU TO STAY HOME. BUT THAT DOESN'T MEAN YOU GET OUT OF DOING THE TALENT SHOW.

YES, MR. TODD.

I KNOW.

NOW, NEWELL... MRS. HENDRICKS TOLD ME THAT AT THE REHEARSAL, IT LOOKED LIKE YOU DIDN'T EVEN HAVE A TALENT TO REHEARSE. I HOPE THAT ISN'T THE CASE.

NO, MR. TODD. I JUST WASN'T FEELING GOOD. I GOT SOMETHING THAT NO ONE ELSE IS EVEN DOING. EVERYONE WILL BE TALKING ABOUT IT ALL WEEKEND LONG, FOR SURE.

I DON'T SUPPOSE YOU'D CARE TO SHARE WHAT IT IS THAT YOU'RE DOING, DO YOU? OR IS IT A SURPRISE?

BIG SURPRISE FOR SURE!

YOU'RE NOT GONNA WANT TO MISS IT!

GO HOME AND GET SOME REST, NEWELL. YOU HAVE A BIG NIGHT AHEAD OF YOU.

DON'T WORRY, MR. TODD. I WON'T LET YOU DOWN.

187

WHAT?

DON'T YOU SEE, CLARA? IF YOU DIDN'T MAKE NEWELL HAVE TO DRESS UP LIKE A PENGUIN, THEN MARTIN WOULDN'T BE SO UPSET.

AND MARTIN ACTUALLY WANTED TO BE A PENGUIN.

SQUEAKY SQUEAK SQUEAKY

I'M GONNA LEAVE THIS RIGHT HERE.

IN CASE YOU NEED REMINDING WHERE CLARA STANDS IN THE LEVEL OF ANNOYANCE.

SQUEAKY SQUEAK SQUEAK!!

SQUEAK

YEESH!

WHAT'S THE BIG DEAL? IT'S NOT LIKE THERE'S A RULE THAT MARTIN CAN'T DRESS UP LIKE A STUPID PENGUIN IF HE WANTED TO.

CLARA'S LEVEL OF ANNOYANCE

EVIL GENIUS

BRATTY

ANNOYING

BOSSY

OKAY, I'LL SEE YOU GUYS.

I NEED TO FIGURE THINGS OUT.

OH, NEWELL, WAIT UP!

WHAT'S UP, SKYLER?

YEAH...

HEY.

I HOPE THAT YOU START FEELING BETTER AND EVERYTHING.

AND I KNOW THAT YOU'RE GONNA FIND SOMETHING AWESOME TO DO FOR THE SHOW TOMORROW NIGHT.

UNLESS GETTING SICK WAS THE TALENT YOU WERE GONNA PERFORM.

HA HA. YEAH, ME NEITHER.

WHICH I WOULDN'T RECOMMEND. HA! HA!

I WOULDN'T WORRY ABOUT MARTIN EITHER. HE'LL GET OVER IT....

ANYWAY...

I FEEL BAD ABOUT WHAT I SAID EARLIER THIS MORNING. I WAS STUPID.

I JUST... I DON'T KNOW WHAT I'M TRYING TO SAY.

HEY...I ALWAYS SAY STUPID THINGS IN THE MORNINGS. I FEEL BAD TOO. IF THAT MEANS ANYTHING.

YEAH?

COOL.

I MEAN, COOL THAT WE'RE OKAY, NOT COOL THAT YOU FELT BAD TOO. HA HA!

GOOD LUCK! FEEL BETTER! AND WE'LL SEE YOU TOMORROW FOR THE SHOW!

SEE YA, SKYLER! YOU BET!

AAAAAAH!

SMOOTH OPERATION ON THE RECOVERY, NEWELL!

SO HERE'S WHAT YOU NEED TO DO, MISTER.

WHAT'S THAT, DAD?

YOU'RE SPENDING TOO MUCH TIME WORRYING ABOUT WHAT'S IN FRONT OF YOU AND ABOUT WHAT YOU CAN'T DO.

YEAH...SO? ISN'T THAT HOW WALLOWERS ARE SUPPOSED TO WALLOW?

BUT WALLOWING MEANS YOU'RE JUST WADING IN THE POOL OF GUNK YOU DON'T WANT TO BE IN IN THE FIRST PLACE. YOU NEED TO GET OUT OF IT SO YOU CAN FIGURE SOMETHING OUT.

BY THE WAY, MY DAD LIKES TO SPEAK IN METAPHORS.

IT'S LIKE WHEN YOU ACCIDENTALLY DRIVE ON A PATCH OF ICE. YOUR FIRST INSTINCT IS TO STEER AWAY FROM IT, RIGHT?

UH-OH!

SKRT!

BUT IF YOU TRY TO STEER OUT OF IT, YOU'LL ONLY SPIN MORE AND GET YOURSELF INTO A DEEPER MESS.

SKRRRRT!

THIS IS NOT GOOD!

FART.

CHAPTER ELEVEN
THE TALENT SHOW

WHAT'S IT LOOK LIKE OUT THERE?

IT'S STARTING TO FILL UP.

AND SO FAR THE ONLY EMBARRASSING THING IS WATCHING MY DAD MESS WITH AN ANCIENT VIDEO CAMERA.

HEY, NEWELL!

WHAT'S THE DEAL WITH THIS PAPER? WHAT AM I SUPPOSED TO DO WITH IT? I DIDN'T SIGN UP FOR THIS!

WELL. I DIDN'T SIGN UP FOR ANY OF THIS, CLARA! I THINK IT'S THE LEAST YOU CAN DO.

JUST FOLLOW MY CUE. YOU'LL FIGURE IT OUT.

EYE ROLL

WHATEVER.

ANNNND WHAT'S THIS? YOU LOOK MORE LIKE A SHABBY DETECTIVE THAN A PENGUIN! DO I NEED TO LET MR. TODD KNOW ABOUT THIS?

IT'S NOTHING FOR YOU TO WORRY ABOUT, CLARA. YOU JUST WORRY ABOUT THOSE NATURAL CURLS OF YOURS.

I'D SAY, "BREAK A LEG." BUT WHAT FUN WOULD THAT BE? GOOD LUCK, NEWELL!

OH YEAH?! WELL, SAY HI TO... YOU KNOW. THAT ONE PLAY!

WHAT'S THE NAME OF THAT ONE SHAKESPEARE PLAY THAT IS BAD LUCK TO SAY IN A THEATER? HAMLET OR SOMETHING?

WHY ARE YOU LOOKING AT ME? I DON'T KNOW.

SAY HI TO HAMLET, CLARA! AND SEE WHAT HAPPENS!

IT'S THE SCOTTISH PLAY, YOU DOPE!!

BAH!

⋯

THE SCOTTISH PLAY?

WHY WOULD A SHAKESPEARE SCOTTISH PLAY BE BAD LUCK TO SAY IN THE THEATER?

I THINK I CAN TELL YOU IN ONE WORD.

WHAT'S THAT?

BAGPIPES.

197

OH, HEY THERE, MR. TODD! YEAH...YOU KNOW, WINGING IT! IT'S US WAITING IN THE WINGS OF THE THEATER BEFORE WE GO ON. YOU KNOW. WINGING IT!

"WINGING IT" HUH? IN ALL MY YEARS INVOLVED WITH THE THEATER, I'VE NEVER HEARD THAT EXPRESSION.

UH...YEAH. WELL... TO BE HONEST, I KINDA MADE IT UP DURING REHEARSAL THE OTHER DAY. YOU KNOW...

WE'RE WINGING IT BACK HERE! HA-HA!

NEWELL...

I LOVE IT!

I'LL ONLY BE ABLE TO WING IT FOR A MOMENT BEFORE GOING OUT THERE.

YOU GUYS HAVE A FULL HOUSE!

ALL RIGHT, BREAK A LEG, BOYS, AND HAVE FUN! I'M ESPECIALLY LOOKING FORWARD TO SEEING YOUR PERFORMANCE TONIGHT, NEWELL.

YOU WON'T BE DISAPPOINTED, MR. TODD!

HE WON'T BE DISAPPOINTED, WILL HE?

THERE'S ONLY ONE WAY TO FIND OUT NOW, ISN'T THERE?

THAT'S NOT MAKING ME FEEL ANY BETTER.

GOOD EVENING, EVERYONE!

BUT IF IT WERE ANYONE ELSE WINGING IT I MIGHT BE CONCERNED. BUT I'M STRANGELY CONFIDENT IN YOUR WINGING ABILITIES.

THANKS, PAL. I APPRECIATE IT.

I SAY THAT WITH THE UNDERSTANDING THAT THE REHEARSAL WAS JUST A FLUKE.

IT'S UNDERSTOOD.

THANK YOU FOR COMING OUT ON SUCH AN HISTORIC OCCASION!

YOU KNOW...I WAS FEELING PRETTY GOOD ABOUT EVERYTHING. BUT THEN WHEN MR. TODD STARTED TALKING TO THE AUDIENCE IT ALL SUDDENLY SEEMED REALLY REAL.

BLAH BLAH BLAH BLAH

AND I WAS STARTING TO DOUBT EVERYTHING I WAS PLANNING TO DO.

BLAH BLAH BLAH

I TRIED TO LOOK OUT INTO THE AUDIENCE.

BUT LUCKILY I COULDN'T SEE TOO MUCH BUT SHADOWS AND LIGHTS.

FLUTTER!

AND THEN I COULD FEEL THE BUTTERFLIES START TO FLUTTER AROUND IN MY STOMACH...

I HOPE I WASN'T GONNA GET SICK ON STAGE AGAIN.

AND WHEN HE INTRODUCED MAX, THE BUTTERFLIES SEEMED TO ESCAPE AND MULTIPLY.

CLAP CLAP CLAP CLAP CLAP CLAP CLAP CLAP

EVEN THOUGH I WANTED TO SEE HOW MY FRIENDS WERE DOING, I REALIZED THAT IF I DIDN'T WANT TO PSYCH MYSELF OUT, I NEEDED TO STEP AWAY AND NOT WATCH

ANY MORE. BECAUSE IT WAS LIKE THE BUTTERFLIES IN MY STOMACH WERE GEARING UP TO MIGRATE TO MEXICO FOR THE WINTER.

OOOF!

I COULDN'T SEE ANYTHING THAT THEY WERE DOING, BUT I COULD STILL HEAR HOW AWESOME THE CROWD REACTED.

THEY LOVED LILLY'S GRACE. I MEAN, WHO WOULDN'T?

I COULD HEAR THEM LAUGHING AT SKYLER JUGGLING THE RUBBER CHICKENS.

THEY APPLAUDED CLARA'S MONOLOGUE FROM HENRY V.

MR. TODD CALLED WHAT'S-HER-NAME'S TAP DANCING PREAMBLE A SHOWSTOPPER. WHATEVER THAT IS.

AND COLLIN KNOCKED IT OUT WITH HIS SONG. THEY ATE IT UP.

I WAS HAPPY FOR ALL OF THEM, BUT I KNEW THAT WITH EACH PERFORMANCE I WAS CLOSER TO MY TIME. IN FACT...

MY TIME WAS UP.

BRING!!

NEWELL? YOU'RE UP, BUDDY.

I UNDERSTAND.

AS I HEADED TO THE STAGE MY HEART WAS PRACTICALLY BEATING OUT OF MY CHEST.

HE'S ON HIS WAY.

IT WAS LIKE HEADING STRAIGHT INTO THE FIRING SQUAD OR SOMETHING. THEY COULD HAVE AT LEAST GIVEN ME A BLINDFOLD.

THANK YOU, COLLIN! I HAVE NEVER HEARD AN EIGHTIES MEDLEY QUITE LIKE THAT BEFORE!

AND UP NEXT! PUTTING THE MISTER IN MYSTERY IS NEWELL! HE'S BACKSTAGE WINGING IT RIGHT NOW. AND WITH THE EXCEPTION OF AN ECCENTRIC COSTUME, EVEN WE DON'T KNOW WHAT'S UP HIS SLEEVE.

SO LET'S PUT OUR HANDS TOGETHER FOR NEWELL!

CLAP! CLAP! CLAP!

SO WHAT'S HE GONNA DO?

I HAVE NO IDEA.

NOTICE HOW I HAVE POPCORN FOR THIS ONE.

THIS IS GOING TO BE FANTASTIC. BWAHAHA

MUNCH MUNCH MUNCH

WITHOUT FURTHER ADO: NEWELL!

CLAP! CLAP! CLAP! CLAP! CLAP!

CLAP! CLAP! CLAP!

...

CLAP! CLAP! CLAP! CLAP!

YOU KNOW THAT MOMENT WHEN YOU HAVE TO STAND IN FRONT OF THE CLASS TO GIVE AN ORAL REPORT?

WELL, LET ME FILL YOU IN ON SOMETHING.

CLAP! CLAP! CLAP! CLAP! CLAP! CLAP CLAP! CLAP CLAP CLAP! CLAP! CLAP!

THIS WAS A LITTLE MORE NERVE-RACKING.

COUGH COUGH

HO' BOY.

I GOT FIVE BUCKS THAT HE SPEWS ALL OVER THE FRONT ROW.

STOP IT, CLARA! HE'S GOT THIS.

AHEM... THANK YOU, MR. TODD. IT'S GREAT TO BE HERE.

WELCOME, EVERYBODY. I HOPE YOU'RE HAVING A GOOD TIME!

WOO!

WEBSTER'S DICTIONARY DEFINES TALENT AS: A SPECIAL ACTION, OFTEN ATHLETIC, CREATIVE, OR ARTISTIC APTITUDE.

AND BY THAT DEFINITION, WE'VE SEEN A LOT OF TALENT HERE TONIGHT.

AM I RIGHT? LET'S GIVE THEM ANOTHER HAND!

CLAP CLAP CLAP CLAP CLAP

WHAT'S THAT KID UP TO?

I DON'T KNOW...BUT I DON'T THINK I LIKE IT.

CLAP CLAP CLAP CLAP CLAP CLAP CLAP

THIS ISN'T STARTING WELL, IS IT?

IT CAN STILL WORK.

MAN...THIS IS A TRAIN WRECK ALREADY. I'M GLAD I HAVE A GOOD VIEW!

MUNCH MUNCH MUNCH

CLAP CLAP CLAP CLAP CLAP CLAP CLAP

OKAY, I ADMIT IT. I DIDN'T WANT TO BE HERE TONIGHT. BUT IT WAS EITHER BE HERE OR SUMMER SCHOOL. SO OUT OF THE TWO, THIS WAS THE BETTER CHOICE. THE ONLY THING WAS THAT I HAD TO WEAR A PARTICULAR COSTUME.

SHOW US!

OH, DON'T ACT LIKE YOU DON'T WANT TO SEE IT TOO!

SHOW US!

SO I WAS REQUIRED TO BE DRESSED UP LIKE A PENGUIN WEARING A TUTU. HA HA HA DO YOU GUYS WANT TO SEE?

WOOO! CLAP CLAP CLAP CLAP CLAP

WHAT?!

YOU'D BE AMAZED AT HOW HARD IT WAS TO FIND A PENGUIN SUIT IN MY SIZE. LUCKILY MY DAD FOUND THIS ONE. I THINK IT WORKS, DON'T YOU THINK?

A TUXEDO? THAT'S NOT WHAT I MEANT, AND YOU KNOW IT!

WEARING A PENGUIN SUIT LIKE THIS MAKES ME FEEL ALL SUAVE AND DEBONAIR. THIS IS PROBABLY WHAT JAMES BOND FEELS LIKE EVERY DAY. HAHA.

WELL...MINUS THE WHOLE TUTU THING, THAT IS.

OKAY... SO I HAD THE PENGUIN SUIT, I HAD THE TUTU, BUT I WAS STILL MISSING THE TALENT TO PERFORM.

THAT'S WHERE THINGS GOT STICKY.

NEWELL'S TALENT IS OFFICIALLY THE LONGEST OF THE NIGHT SO FAR.

GRUMBLE

HE'S TRYING TO TALK HIS WAY OUT OF IT, I SEE.

I WAS RACKING MY BRAIN TRYING TO FIGURE OUT SOMETHING—ANYTHING— FOR ME TO DO! COLLIN AND I EVEN WENT UP TO THE ATTIC TO SEE IF ANY OF MY DAD'S OLD STUFF COULD HELP.

OKAY, COLLIN! OPEN THE CURTAIN!

YOU GOT IT!

A QUICK SHOUTOUT TO MY DAD, WHO HELPED GET ALL OF THIS OUT HERE.

HE'S THE ONE WITH THE ANTIQUE VIDEO CAMERA OVER THERE.

WHURRRRR

OKAY... THIS THING IS GETTING OLD.

WHY IS HE TAKING THE TUTU OFF? HE CAN'T DO THAT!

I DON'T THINK THERE WAS ANYTHING THAT SAID HE HAD TO KEEP THE TUTU ON THE ENTIRE TIME.

HEY! PUT THE TUTU BACK ON!

SO AFTER WE GOT THE BOXES DOWN, I DIVED INTO THEM. TRYING TO FIGURE OUT IF THERE WAS ANYTHING I COULD USE.

TOSS!

I TRIED MY HAND AT MAGIC.

BUT IT WAS A BUST.

FLUH-FLUH FLAP!

I EVEN TRIED PICKING UP THE GUITAR AND PLAYING THAT. I'LL LET YOU DECIDE HOW GOOD I AM AT IT.

AND THAT'S EVEN AFTER NINETY MINUTES OF PRACTICE ON MY FRONT PORCH. YOU WOULD HAVE THOUGHT I WOULD HAVE GOTTEN BETTER, RIGHT?

THEN I REALIZED THAT WHILE I LIKE LISTENING TO GUITAR MUSIC, I DIDN'T HAVE ANY REAL INTEREST IN PLAYING IT. AND MAYBE THERE WAS A LINK BETWEEN SOMEONE'S NATURAL ABILITY AND SOMEONE'S NATURAL INTEREST IN IT.

EVERYONE THAT YOU'VE SEEN TONIGHT HAS BOTH A NATURAL ABILITY AND A NATURAL INTEREST IN THEIR TALENT.

TWANG!

I TOLD YOU THE NEIGHBOR KID WAS GOING TO PLAY THAT THING, HAROLD!

MY EARS! MY EARS!

AND I'M WILLING TO BET THAT THEY DIDN'T START WORKING ON IT JUST A COUPLE OF DAYS AGO. BUT THAT THEY'VE BEEN WORKING HARD ON IT FOR A LONG TIME.

PICASSO DIDN'T START OUT AS PICASSO. JOHN WILLIAMS, THE COMPOSER, DIDN'T START OUT AS THE JOHN WILLIAMS. THEY HAD AN INTEREST IN THEIR ART, AND THROUGH HARD WORK THEY BECAME GREAT AT IT.

WHO'S PICASSO?

WHO'S JOHN WILLIAMS?

I GUESS I THOUGHT THAT IF I HAD THE TALENT FOR SOMETHING IT WOULD HAVE BEEN AUTOMATIC.

BUT IT'S NOT.

WILL I EVER BE GOOD AT PLAYING THE GUITAR? I DON'T KNOW. BUT IT WOULD HAVE TO BE SOMETHING I WOULD HAVE TO DEVOTE HOURS UPON HOURS TO. AND I DON'T KNOW IF I HAVE A NATURAL INTEREST IN DOING THAT.

SO I'LL HAVE TO JUST APPRECIATE THOSE WHO DO. AND CAN.

SO DO YOU HAVE A TALENT OR NOT, KID?

UM... SPOILERS!

ANYWAY...

HAVE YOU NOTICED THAT THERE ARE SOME PEOPLE OUT THERE WHO HAVE A GREAT TALENT, BUT NOT NECESSARILY ONE THAT CAN BE PERFORMED ON STAGE? IT'S LIKE MY CLASSMATE ROGER. HE HAS A FANTASTIC TALENT OF ALWAYS BEING AROUND WHEN I NEED ADVICE ABOUT GIRLS. WHETHER I WANT IT OR NOT.

HA! YOU'RE WELCOME, DUDE!

SO THAT'S WHEN I CAME UP WITH A NEW PLAN. READY?

IF I COULDN'T FIND MYSELF A TALENT, THEN MAYBE I COULD HELP OTHERS WITH THEIRS.

CAN SOMEBODY SEND MARTIN OUT?

SIGH! WHAT DO YOU WANT, NEWELL?

COME ON OUT HERE FOR A SECOND, WILL YA?

MARTIN WALLACE, EVERYBODY! YOU'LL SEE HIM NEXT, AFTER ME! GIVE HIM SOME ENCOURAGEMENT, WILL YA?

WHAT DO YOU WANT, NEWELL?

CLAP CLAP CLAP CLAP CLAP CLAP CLAP CLAP CLAP CLAP

FOR THE PAST FEW DAYS I'VE WONDERED WHY MARTIN'S BEEN MAD AT ME.

WE'VE NEVER BEEN TIGHT. BUT HE'S NEVER BEEN MAD AT ME. AND THEN I FOUND OUT THAT I TOOK PART OF HIS IDEA FOR THE TALENT SHOW.

I HOPE THIS MAKES UP FOR IT ALL.

?

?

SUSPICIOUS

Zip

WHAT? HA HA!! NO WAY!

IS THIS FOR ME? FOR TONIGHT? CAN I USE IT NOW?

OF COURSE!

HA HA! YES!

NEWELL'S THE ONLY GUY I KNOW WHO CAN LITERALLY THROW UP ON A GUY ONE DAY, AND ON THE VERY NEXT DAY MAKE HIM FEEL LIKE HE'S ON TOP OF THE WORLD.

TALK ABOUT HAVING A TALENT!

THIS NIGHT IS RUINED. NEWELL HASN'T HUMILIATED HIMSELF YET!

THE AUDIENCE LOVES IT.

CLAP CLAP CLAP CLAP CLAP CLAP CLAP! CLAP CLAP!

ALL RIGHT. I THINK HE'S HIJACKED THIS TALENT SHOW LONG ENOUGH.

TIME TO MAKE SOME HUSTLE WITH MY MUSCLE!

THAT'S RIGHT! TAKE THAT KID OUT OF MY TALENT SHOW, PHYLLIS!

AND RIGHT INTO MY SUMMER SCHOOL PROGRAM. BWAHAHA!!

CLAP CLAP CLAP CLAP! CLAP! CLAP! CLAP! CLAP CLAP CLAP CLAP CLAP CLAP CLAP!

211

CHEER!

OKAY, NEWELL. FINE. JUST ONE MORE THING AND WE'LL NEED TO MOVE ON.

ALL RIGHT?

THANKS, MRS. HENDRICKS!

WAIT! I'D LIKE IT IF YOU COULD STICK AROUND, THOUGH.

YOU WANT ME TO STAY?

IF YOU COULD.

SIGH. IF IT SPEEDS THINGS UP, OKAY.

THANKS, MRS. HENDRICKS.

SO...AS I WAS SAYING: SOMETIMES YOU CAN HELP SOMEONE WITH THEIR TALENT, JUST LIKE WITH MARTIN.

BUT SOMETIMES...

SOMETIMES YOU MIGHT BE ABLE TO HELP SOMEONE ACHIEVE A DREAM THEY NEVER THOUGHT WOULD COME TRUE.

AND IF YOU HAVE A CHANCE TO DO THAT FOR SOMEONE, I SAY, 'DO IT.'

IT MIGHT BE AS EASY AS LOOKING IN AN OLD DUSTY BOX. YOU NEVER KNOW WHAT YOU MIGHT FIND.

"RUSTLE RUSTLE!"

YOU MIGHT FIND, LET'S SAY, AN OLD BEAT-UP HAT, LIKE THIS ONE.

AND MAYBE EVEN A BIG STICK AND A FAKE MUSTACHE.

BULLY...

HERE YOU GO, MRS. HENDRICKS.

WAIT... THIS IS FOR ME?!

YOU BET!

BUT I... I DON'T KNOW WHAT TO SAY.

I REMEMBER YOU SAID THAT YOU ALWAYS WANTED TO COSPLAY LIKE TEDDY ROOSEVELT.

HE'S ALWAYS BEEN A HERO OF MINE.

BULLY! HA! HA!

HAHA! THIS IS GREAT!!

YES!

OKAY, MARK. THAT'S OUR CUE.

TAP
TAP
TAP

TAP
TAP
TAP!

GASP! ARE THEY PLAYING "YOU'RE A GRAND OLD FLAG"??!!

THIS IS THE BEST DAY EVER!

THAT NIGHT I, ALONG WITH EVERYONE ELSE IN THE THEATER, WITNESSED MRS. HENDRICKS PROUDLY SING "YOU'RE A GRAND OLD FLAG." SHE KNEW EVERY WORD.

I NEVER THOUGHT I WOULD SAY THIS, BUT SHE TORE THE HOUSE DOWN.

BOY, DID SHE. AND SHE WAS SIMPLY AMAZING.

AND THEN, RIGHT ON CUE.

YOU'RE A GRAND OLD FLAG, YOU'RE A HIGH-FLYING FLAG

IT WAS JUST LIKE ONE OF THOSE MOVIE MUSICALS.

HA!

IT WAS GOING GREAT. BETTER THAN I THOUGHT.

AND FOREVER IN PEACE MAY YOU WAVE

AND THEN MARTIN JOINED IN, AND IT GOT EVEN BETTER.

YOU'RE THE EMBLEM OF THE LAND I LOVE, THE HOME OF THE FREE AND THE BRAVE

EVERY HEART BEATS TRUE

UNDER RED, WHITE & BLUE

WHERE THERE'S NEVER A BOAST OR BRAG

BUT SHOULD OLD ACQUAINTANCE BE FORGOT

AND THEN THE IMPOSSIBLE HAPPENED.

KEEP YOUR EYE ON THE GRAND OLD FLAG!

THE REST OF THE SONG WENT GREAT. THE CROWD CHEERED AND EVEN SANG ALONG.

OKAY...MAYBE NOT SANG. MOST OF THEM DIDN'T KNOW THE SONG. BUT THEY HUMMED. THEY HUMMED A LOT. AND WHEN THE SONG GOT DONE...

APPLAUSE!

EPILOGUE

I DON'T THINK I'VE EVER SEEN MARTIN MOVE THAT FAST BEFORE.

I'M IMPRESSED THAT YOU KEPT HIM IN THE SHOT THE WHOLE TIME.

I THOUGHT THAT WAS PART OF HIS ACT.

EVEN WHEN THE SQUIRREL GOT INTO HIS COSTUME?

HEY, I'VE SEEN ENOUGH PERFORMANCE ART IN MY LIFE TO NOT QUESTION ANYTHING.

HA! PERFORMANCE ART.

SO... LET ME GET THIS STRAIGHT. YOU INADVERTENTLY TOOK MARTIN'S IDEA TO DRESS UP LIKE A PENGUIN.

THEN, AT REHEARSAL, YOU THREW UP ON HIM.

AND AT THE TALENT SHOW, YOU LET A SQUIRREL LOOSE ON HIM.

PRETTY MUCH.

I FEEL LIKE MARTIN HAD A WORSE WEEK THAN I DID.

THE CROWD LOVED IT. TOO BAD HE HAD TO GET THE RABIES SHOTS AFTERWARD.

LET ME ASK YOU THIS: WOULD YOU RATHER GO THROUGH A SERIES OF RABIES SHOTS OR GO TO SUMMER SCHOOL?

THE END

ACKNOWLEDGMENTS

* * *

I WILL ALWAYS BE GRATEFUL FOR THE THREE MAIN PEOPLE IN MY LIFE—WITHOUT THEM, THIS BOOK WOULD NOT BE POSSIBLE. THEIR LOVE, BELIEF, AND SACRIFICES DON'T GO UNNOTICED. MY MOM, KATHRYN, WHO WANTED TO LEARN HOW TO DRAW HERSELF, ALWAYS MADE SURE THAT I HAD PENCILS AND PAPER TO PRACTICE MY CARTOONING. MY WIFE, ERIN, WHO NEVER STOPPED BELIEVING IN ME, AND WHO SLEPT MANY NIGHTS ON THE COUCH NEAR MY STUDIO DESK WHILE I WORKED. AND, OF COURSE, TO MY SON, WYETH. THIS BOOK IS BUILT ON THE ADVENTURES, LOVE, AND LAUGHTER THAT HE AND I HAVE SHARED TOGETHER. BEING HIS DAD IS THE BEST PART OF WHO I AM. I'M A LUCKY MAN TO HAVE THESE THREE IN MY LIFE. THANK YOU.

THANKS TO ALL THE WONDERFUL PEOPLE AT LITTLE, BROWN BOOKS FOR YOUNG READERS WHO HELPED SHAPE THIS GRAPHIC NOVEL, ESPECIALLY TO MY TALENTED EDITOR, AND REALLY GREAT GUY, RUSS BUSSE. AND THANKS TO MY DESIGNER, CHRISTINA QUINTERO, WHO ORGANIZED ALL MY PAGES.

A BIG THANK YOU TO BOTH JODELL SADLER AND JILL CORCORAN. YOUR ENTHUSIASM FOR THIS STORY HELPED ME MORE THAN YOU KNOW. YOU'RE THE BEST AGENTS I COULD HAVE ASKED FOR.

AND, OF COURSE, TO ALL THE FANS OF MY WEBCOMIC, *MISTER & ME*. YOUR DEDICATION TO NEWELL AND HIS DAD HELPED THEM GET HERE. THANK YOU FOR ALL THE LAUGHS.

JASON PLATT IS A PROFESSIONAL CARTOONIST
AND MEMBER OF THE NATIONAL CARTOONISTS SOCIETY.
WHILE BORN IN THE MIDWEST, HE GREW UP IN DURHAM,
NORTH CAROLINA, AND LATER GRADUATED WITH
HONORS FROM THE SAVANNAH COLLEGE OF ART AND
DESIGN, IN SAVANNAH, GEORGIA. IN HIS FREE TIME,
JASON CAN BE FOUND PERFORMING OR WRITING FOR
THE THEATER. JASON LIVES IN DAVENPORT, IOWA,
WITH HIS WIFE, SON, AND CAT.